BOOK THREE

Lucky Days
with
Mr. and Mrs.
Green

KEITH BAKER

Harcourt, Inc.
Orlando   Austin   New York   San Diego   Toronto   London

For Betsy and Chris,
Minna and Cooper,
and their sunshine

www.HarcourtBooks.com

First Harcourt paperback edition 2006

Library of Congress Cataloging-in-Publication Data
Baker, Keith, 1953–
Lucky days with Mr. and Mrs. Green/Keith Baker.
p. cm.
"Book Three."
Summary: Mr. and Mrs. Green, a loving alligator couple, try their hand at detective work, a gumball-guessing contest, and the town talent show.
[1. Lost and found possessions—Fiction. 2. Contests—Fiction. 3. Talent shows—Fiction. 4. Alligators—Fiction. 5. Humorous stories.] I. Title.
PZ7.B17427Mr 2005
[Fic]—dc22 2004005740
ISBN-13: 978-0152-16500-0 ISBN-10: 0-15-216500-2
ISBN-13: 978-0152-05604-9 (pb) ISBN-10: 0-15-205604-1 (pb)

A C E G H F D B
C E G H F D (pb)

Printed in Singapore

The illustrations in this book were done with acrylic paint on illustration board.
The display type was created by Jane Dill Design.
The text type was set in Giovanni Book.
Color separations by Colourscan Co. Pte. Ltd., Singapore
Printed and bound by Tien Wah Press, Singapore
Production supervision by Ginger Boyer
Designed by Keith Baker

Contents

Lost and Found

"They're gone," said Mrs. Green.
"Vanished . . . disappeared . . .
I've looked *everywhere.*"

"I'll help you look!" said Mr. Green.

Detective work was one of his hobbies—
Lost and Found was his specialty.

"Detective Green," he said,
"at your service.
If you can't find it, *I can*.
Satisfaction guaranteed."

Mr. Green felt confident.
He looked like Sherlock Holmes.
"Now tell me," he said,
"what *are* we looking for?"

"Pearls!" said Mrs. Green.

"My necklace *and* my watch."

Mr. Green looked closely.

"AHA!" he said.

"Your pearls *are* gone."

He made a note of it.

"Let's start from the beginning.

Describe these pearls.

Tell me every little detail.

Be precise.

And, above all . . .

stay calm."
(He was more excited
than ever. Mrs. Green
was calm.)

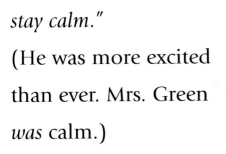

"Well," said Mrs. Green,
"the pearls are white and round—
about the size of blueberries.

The necklace is beautiful.
The watch is beautiful *and*
it tells time.
I wear them both every day."
Mr. Green drew a picture.

"When did you last see
   the pearls?" he asked.
"This morning," she said.
"I took them off in the tub.
   I fell asleep, and when I woke up,
   they were gone."
"AHA!" said Mr. Green.
"Follow me!
   Stay steady, and *stay calm.*"
   (Mrs. Green *was* calm.)

They walked straight to the tub.

"There!" said Mr. Green.

He pointed to a pearly cluster.

But there were no pearls—only bubbles.

"We must be close," said Mr. Green.

"I can feel it, and—AHA!—I can see it."

Mr. Green pointed to a lump under the rug.

But it was just his rubber duck.

"Let's move on," said Mr. Green.

"I have lots of ideas, loads of experience,
and tons of time."

They looked in the toaster.
No pearls—only crumbs
and three raisins.

They looked in the slippers.
No pearls—only peanut
shells and a paper clip.

They looked in the laundry.
No pearls—only socks and
candy wrappers.

They looked in the vase.
No pearls—only flowers
and a Ping-Pong ball.

"Detective work can be
challenging at times,"
said Mr. Green.
"*This* is one of those times.

Stay steady,
stay by my side,
and, above all, *stay calm.*"
(Mrs. Green *was* calm.)

They looked in the toolbox.
No pearls—only tools
and chocolate bars.

They looked in the brush bucket.
No pearls—only brushes
and banana peels.

They looked in the pillow.
No pearls—only feathers
and potato chips.

They looked in the cookie jar.
No pearls—only cookies
and the house keys.

The cookies were one of Mr. Green's
favorites—*jumbo*. (He also liked
small, medium, and large.)

"Cookie?" asked Mr. Green.

"I'd love one," said Mrs. Green.

Mr. Green grabbed a handful.

(Cookies helped him concentrate.)

Together they studied his notes.

Where could those pearls be?

They both sat down to think.

Mr. Green ate another cookie.

And another. And another.

"I can't concentrate," he said.

"Me neither," said Mrs. Green.

"The crows are too noisy.

They've been noisy all morning long—

ever since I took my bath."

"Are *you* thinking what *I'm* thinking?"
he asked.

"I think so!" she said.

They rushed out to the garage.

Then they rushed back to the house.

Mrs. Green climbed up the ladder.

Mr. Green held it steady.

(He was afraid of heights.)

"Here they are!"
said Mrs. Green.
"My necklace *and*
my watch."

"Are you *positively* sure?"
asked Mr. Green.
"Posi-pearl-tively,"
she said.

Mr. Green looked closely.

Every pearl was in its place.

"Case solved," he said.

He made a note of it.

Then he closed the notebook.

But his detective work was not

yet finished—

there were still more cookies.

And Mr. Green was positively certain

he could find them all.

Gumballs

"Look," said Mrs. Green.

"A gumball-guessing contest!
I've never *seen* so many gumballs."

"I've never *imagined* so many,"
said Mr. Green.

Mr. Green loved
gumballs.
To win them all
would be a dream
come true.

"Let's guess!"
said Mrs. Green.
"This could be
our lucky day."

She quickly wrote down a number.

Mr. Green *really*
wanted to win.
He needed more
than luck.
He needed math.

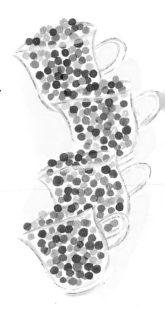

He began calculating.

19 gumballs in a cup . . .

2 cups in a pint . . .

2 pints in a quart . . .

4 quarts in a gallon . . .

about 25 gallons

in the gumball jar . . .

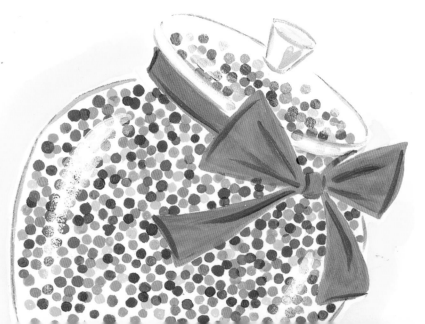

So . . . 19 x 2 x 2 x 4 x 25 = 7,600.

Plus 317 (his favorite number)

for a grand total of 7,917.

Mr. Green wrote down his calculation.

The winners would be announced soon.

On the way home, Mr. Green imagined
gumballs everywhere—

gumball fountains,

gumball trees,

and a gumball car with gumball tires.

The world had never looked so wonderful.

At home, Mr. Green stretched out for a nap.

Mrs. Green began to paint—

she was inspired by all the gumball colors.

While she painted . . .

Mr. Green tossed and turned in his sleep.

He had a strange and crazy dream—

a spotty,
polka-dotty

gumball dream.

He was floating through a gumball galaxy . . .

without gravity (but with Mrs. Green by his side).

Suddenly, Mr. Green woke up—

someone was knocking at the door.

"CONGRATULATIONS!"

"You—yes, YOU,"

said the delivery man,

"are the Gumball-Guessing Champion!

I am pleased to present your prize—"

"Seven thousand nine hundred
and seventeen gumballs!"

"Yippee!
  Hooray!
  Yahooooo!"
said Mr. Green.
"And thank you!
  It's a dream
  come true."

Mrs. Green came running in—
she had heard all the excitement.

"I won first prize!" said Mr. Green.

"Congratulations," said Mrs. Green.

"How did you do it?"

"Math," said Mr. Green. "Lots of it.
And a little luck."

"Mrs. Green," said the delivery man,
"you are a gumball-guessing winner, too!
I am pleased to present you
the third-place prize—
and *heeeeeeerrrrrrreee* it is!"

Inside was a little goldfish.

(He was one of Mrs. Green's

favorite colors—gold.)

"Congratulations!" said Mr. Green.

"What will you name him?"

"Gumball," said Mrs. Green.

"*Sir Gumball Goldfish the First.*

I can't wait to paint his portrait.

What will you do with *your* prize?"

"Oh, I have an idea," he said.

"Follow me."

"Look out below," said Mrs. Green.

"Here I come!"

"Goldfish and gumballs!" said Mr. Green.

"This really *is* our lucky day."

The Talent Show

Mr. Green turned up the water.
He sang louder—and louder—and *louder!*
No one could hear him sing
in the shower.

Except for Mrs. Green.

She loved listening to him.

He sang all sorts of songs.

(Mrs. Green especially enjoyed opera.)

Every year, Mr. Green performed in the Talent Show.
He had played . . .

the harmonica,   the tuba,

the bongos,   and the triangle.

But this year he would sing.

He had been practicing in the shower every day.

He was ready—

the Talent Show was that afternoon.

Mr. and Mrs. Green hurried to the show.

They watched and waited.

They enjoyed all the performers, especially . . .

the baton twirler
(three batons
at once!),

the ballet dancers
(graceful as swans!),

and the storyteller
(a little Shakespeare,
a lot of Dr. Seuss!).

But their favorite performers of all were the magician and his assistant.

Mr. and Mrs. Green wanted to try this trick at home.

(It would take a lot of practice.)

Finally, it was Mr. Green's turn.

He walked onto the stage.

He was not nervous—just excited.

So was Mrs. Green.
*What song
would he sing?*

Mr. Green stood still and tall.

He waited for silence.

He waited for inspiration.

He waited to feel the music inside.

Then he took a deep breath and began.

But when he opened his mouth,

nothing came out—

not a note or a noise,

not a peep or a pip,

not a squeak or a squawk.

Mr. Green was soundless.

Soundless . . . songless . . . speechless.

Mr. Green took another deep breath.

He began once more. Again, nothing.

Something was wrong, very wrong.

Oh dear, thought Mrs. Green.

She got an idea.

She ran behind the stage.

She turned on the hose.

She sprayed water over the curtain.

On the other side, the water fell on Mr. Green.

Soon he was completely soaked.

He felt wet.

He felt comfortable.

He felt at home.

He felt like . . .

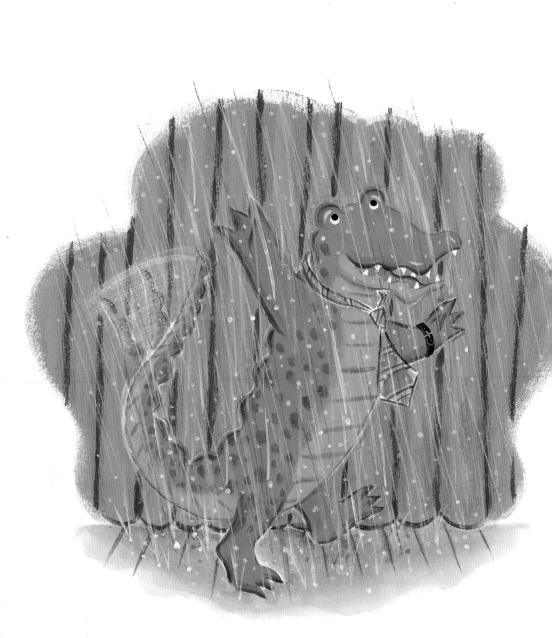

SINGING!

Mr. Green sang loudly
(with enthusiasm and energy),

he sang softly
(with feeling and emotion),

and then he made up a song
(with a snappy beat—
he was *in the groove*).

When Mr. Green finished, he took a bow.

The audience clapped wildly—

even those who got wet.

They shouted, "*Bravo!*"

(*Bravo* means "hooray" in Italian.)

Mr. Green bowed again.

Then he hurried off to find Mrs. Green.

"Thank you!" said Mr. Green.

"That water did the trick!"

"You're welcome," said Mrs. Green.

"You always sing best

when you're soaking wet."

"I'll need your help again

next year," he said.

"Singing?" she asked.

"No," said Mr. Green.

"Dancing . . . the tango . . .

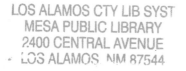

on roller skates!"